Dear Parent:
Your child's love of re... robo

Every child learns to read in a diffe..... ...., ... own speed. Some go back and forth between reading levels and read favorite books again and again. Others read through each level in order. You can help your young reader improve and become more confident by encouraging his or her own interests and abilities. From books your child reads with you to the first books he or she reads alone, there are I Can Read Books for every stage of reading:

SHARED READING
Basic language, word repetition, and whimsical illustrations, ideal for sharing with your emergent reader

BEGINNING READING
Short sentences, familiar words, and simple concepts for children eager to read on their own

READING WITH HELP
Engaging stories, longer sentences, and language play for developing readers

READING ALONE
Complex plots, challenging vocabulary, and high-interest topics for the independent reader

ADVANCED READING
Short paragraphs, chapters, and exciting themes for the perfect bridge to chapter books

I Can Read Books have introduced children to the joy of reading since 1957. Featuring award-winning authors and illustrators and a fabulous cast of beloved characters, I Can Read Books set the standard for beginning readers.

A lifetime of discovery begins with the magical words **"I Can Read!"**

Visit www.icanread.com for information
on enriching your child's reading experience.

HarperCollins®, ☎®, and I Can Read Book® are trademarks of HarperCollins Publishers.

Transformers: Robot Roll Call
HASBRO and its logo, TRANSFORMERS and all related characters are trademarks of Hasbro and are used with permission.
© 2008 Hasbro. All Rights Reserved.
Printed in the United States of America.
No part of this book may be used or reproduced in any manner whatsoever without written permission except in the case of brief
quotations embodied in critical articles and reviews. For information address HarperCollins Children's Books, a division of
HarperCollins Publishers, 1350 Avenue of the Americas, New York, NY 10019.
www.icanread.com
Library of Congress catalog card number: 2007933219
ISBN 978-0-06-088808-4
1   2   3   4   5   6   7   8   9   10
❖
First Edition

ROBOT ROLL CALL
Story by Jennifer Frantz

HarperCollins*Publishers*

The Autobots are strangers in a strange,
new land—planet Earth.

In this new world,

the Autobots try their best

to blend in.

Sometimes it is easy to stay off the radar. But sometimes the Autobots have a hard time keeping a low profile.

All the Autobots

look up to **Optimus Prime**.

He is a brave leader

and a true friend.

When one of his friends

is in trouble,

his trusty tools

come to the rescue.

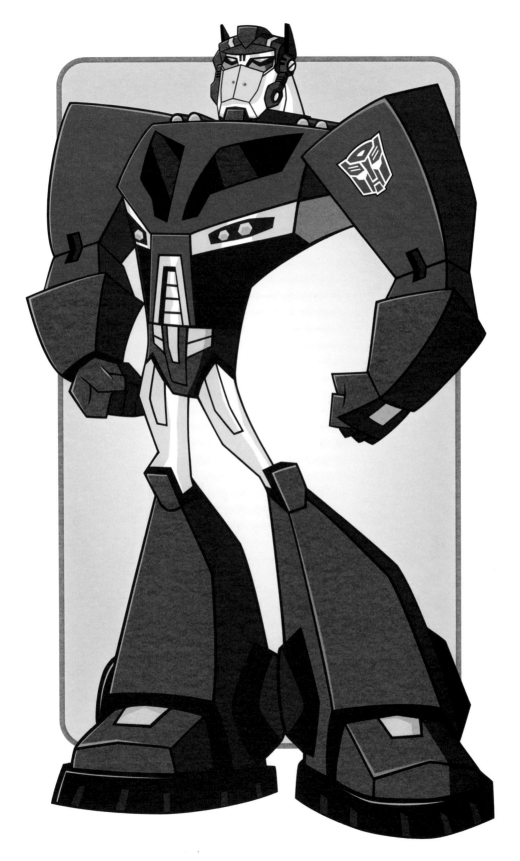

Bulkhead is a gentle giant.

But the bad guys should watch out!

This big bot can bust things up.

11

Bumblebee thinks Earth
is the place to be.
It's fast, fun,
and flashy.
Just like he is!

Bumblebee is always ready for action.

His stinger blasts

can stun anything

in his path.

Prowl loves to look at nature.

And just like a cat,

he is always

ready to pounce.

With his super senses and sneaky moves,
Prowl can creep up on any enemy.

Ratchet is one

of the oldest Autobots.

He can be gruff and tough,

but is always there

for a bot in need.

Ratchet uses

his magnetic powers

and medical skills

to patch up fallen friends.

Sari Sumdac loves
to hang out with her
Autobot pals.
And her special energy key
can heal bots hurt in battle.

Sari's dad, **Isaac**,
is a robot scientist.
Busy and curious,
his mind is always
on his work.

The Autobots are not the only ones

new to planet Earth.

Megatron is the leader

of the Decepticons.

He wants

to control the Allspark,

the source of all energy.

First he must

stop the Autobots,

and anyone else

who stands in his way.

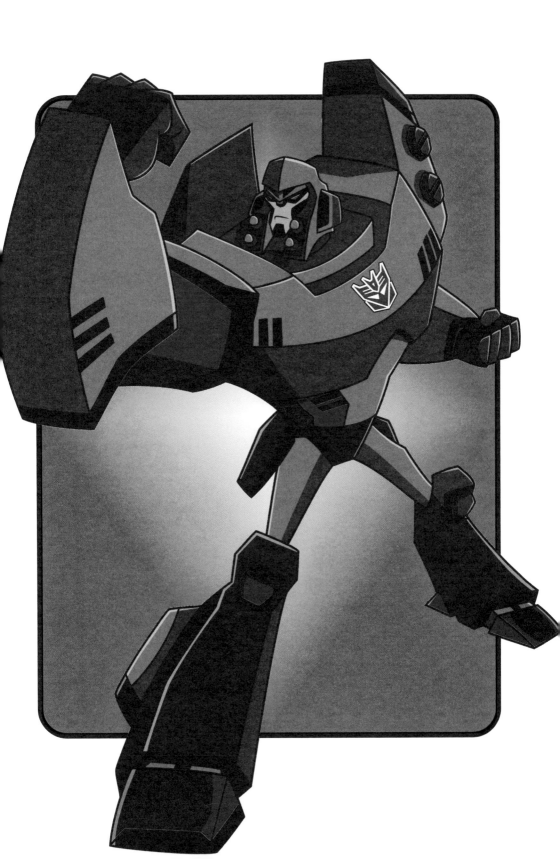

Starscream is fast,
fierce, and full of lies.
No one can trust him,
not even the other
Decepticons.
He streaks
onto the scene
and sends out
a supersonic scream.

Blackarachnia

is loyal to
only one
Decepticon—
herself.

Any bot who falls under her spell

will get stung with her venom.

A sly robot hunter,

Lockdown will work

for anyone,

if the price is right.

No bot wants

to get snared

in his deadly net.

Lugnut is a supersized threat!

This bomb-blasting brute

is as wild as a pit bull.

And he will fight to the end
for his master, Megatron.

The Autobots and the Decepticons
are powerful forces.

No one knows what will happen
when they face off.

Planet Earth

will never be the same!